THE
PRICE
OF
FREEDOM

HOW ONE TOWN STOOD UP TO SLAVERY

JUDITH BLOOM FRADIN *and* DENNIS BRINDELL FRADIN

ILLUSTRATED BY ERIC VELASQUEZ

WALKER BOOKS FOR YOUNG READERS
AN IMPRINT OF BLOOMSBURY
NEW YORK LONDON NEW DELHI SYDNEY

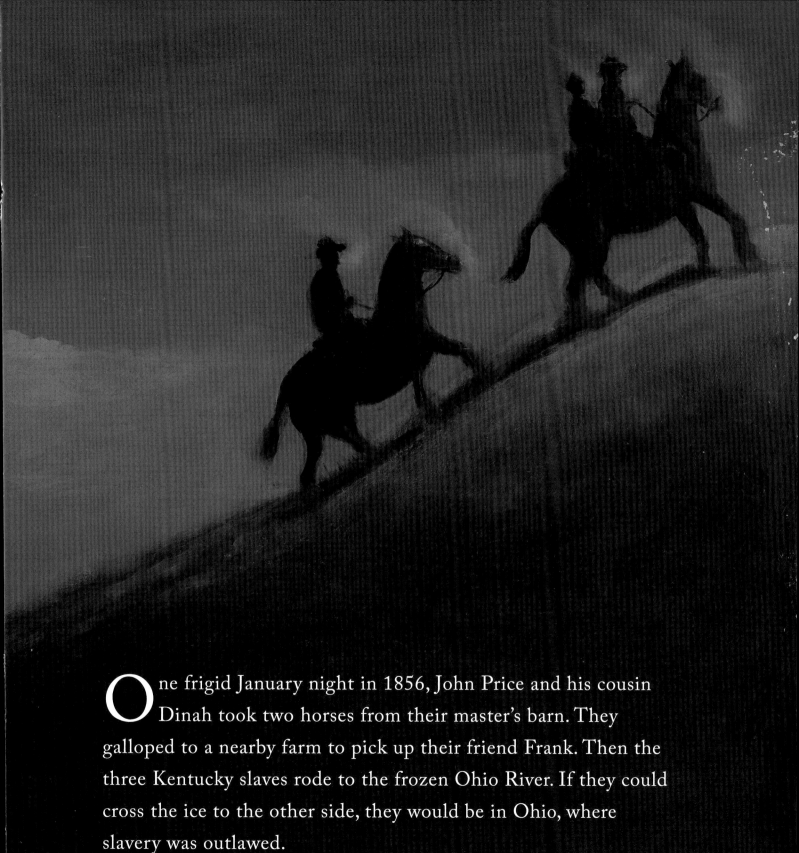

One frigid January night in 1856, John Price and his cousin
Dinah took two horses from their master's barn. They
galloped to a nearby farm to pick up their friend Frank. Then the
three Kentucky slaves rode to the frozen Ohio River. If they could
cross the ice to the other side, they would be in Ohio, where
slavery was outlawed.

They rode across the ice safely but ran into trouble at the Ohio shore. In the darkness they couldn't find a way up the icy riverbank. The three runaway slaves searched all night but didn't spot a path until dawn. By the time they scrambled onto the free soil of Ohio, their hands and feet were numb with cold.

A short way into Ohio, they met an elderly Quaker. The runaways needed help getting off the horses, which immediately ran back home across the frozen river. The Quaker gentleman then led the three fugitive slaves to his house and sheltered them for two weeks.

When they had recovered from their journey, the trio split up, perhaps to confuse slave hunters searching for two men and a woman. Dinah went off alone. John and Frank traveled northward together, mostly at night, usually on foot, always following the North Star. They moved slowly, for John had a deformed foot that made walking through the ice, snow, and mud terribly painful.

But move they must. Six years earlier, Congress had passed the Fugitive Slave Act of 1850. It allowed slave owners to capture runaways anywhere on US soil—even in free states like Ohio—and made aiding escaped slaves a federal crime. The only truly safe place for fugitive slaves was Canada, which had ended

John and Frank received help on their journey. Some people, such as the elderly Quaker, defied the Fugitive Slave Act by turning their homes into Underground Railroad "stations." These rest stops for runaway slaves were located about every ten miles. Each night the two friends continued northward. Each morning they sought shelter for the day at an Underground Railroad station.

After a few weeks, John and Frank reached Lake Erie. There they learned that they could not yet go to Canada, because ice in the lake was blocking boat traffic. They decided to spend the rest of the winter in one of the nation's busiest Underground Railroad stops: Oberlin, Ohio—about two hundred miles from where they started.

Oberlin College professors and the town's ministers claimed there was a "higher law" than the Fugitive Slave Act. This was the law of right and wrong, by which everyone deserved to be free. Between the 1830s and the 1850s, Oberlinians sheltered three thousand runaway slaves. Many of the slaves felt so safe and welcome in the town that they settled there instead of moving on to Canada. By the 1850s, about four hundred of Oberlin's two thousand residents were African Americans, most of them escaped slaves.

While they waited for the ice to clear, John lodged with a farmer and Frank lived nearby. Both men worked at odd jobs. By spring the two friends liked Oberlin so much that they decided to stay there.

Trouble began in early September 1858, when a ten-year-old boy spied several "rough-looking" men on the porch of an Oberlin flophouse. Suspecting that they were slave hunters, Oberlinians posted lookouts around the hotel.

Indeed, the men *were* slave hunters. They were led by Anderson Jennings, a Kentuckian who had been promised $500 per slave (equal to about $13,000 each in today's money) for returning John and Frank to their former owners.

On Sunday, September 12, Jennings visited the Boyntons, one of the area's few families that favored the Fugitive Slave Law. He offered thirteen-year-old Shakespeare Boynton $20 to help him capture the two runaways.

The next morning, Shake Boynton drove a horse and buggy to the farm where John Price lived. He asked if John and Frank wanted to earn some money digging potatoes.

John told Shake he couldn't because he had to take care of Frank, who was recovering from an injury. However, another friend of his might want the job. John went with Shake to show him where this friend lived.

John and young Shake Boynton were traveling along a dirt road when three of Jennings's accomplices pulled up next to them. The men pulled their guns on John. "I'll go with you," he said, realizing that resisting would be useless.

The slave hunters drove John toward Wellington, a town nine miles south of Oberlin. As the carriage passed a cemetery, John noticed a tall, bearded Oberlin College student walking along the road. John shouted that he was being kidnapped, but the young man didn't seem to hear him.

2:30 p.m.

After Shake reported to Anderson Jennings and pocketed his reward, Jennings headed to Wellington. He holed up with his accomplices and John Price in the attic of Wadsworth's Hotel. A southbound train was due in Wellington at 5:13 p.m. Jennings planned to board that train with John Price, return John to his master, and claim his $500 reward.

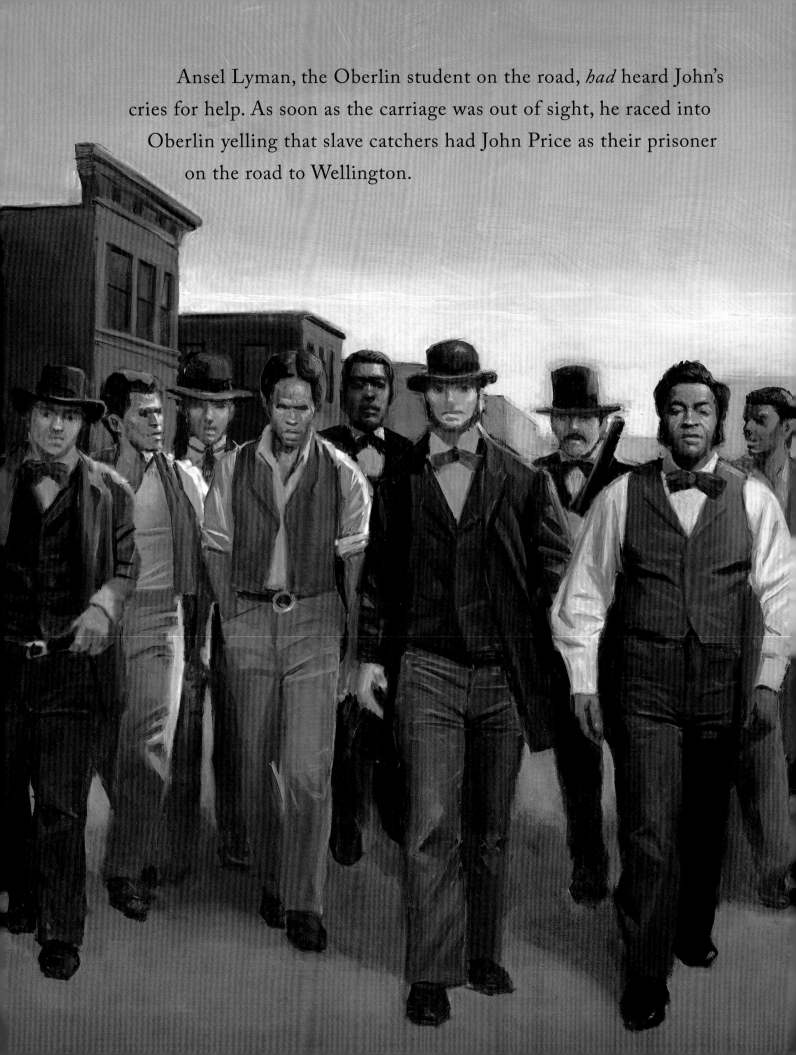

Ansel Lyman, the Oberlin student on the road, *had* heard John's cries for help. As soon as the carriage was out of sight, he raced into Oberlin yelling that slave catchers had John Price as their prisoner on the road to Wellington.

Within minutes, hundreds of Oberlinians set out for Wellington. Farmers, shopkeepers, and ministers hurried off to rescue John Price. So did Oberlin College professors and students. Young and old, men and women, fathers and sons, black and white, armed and unarmed—people jammed the roads in carts and buggies, on foot, and on horseback.

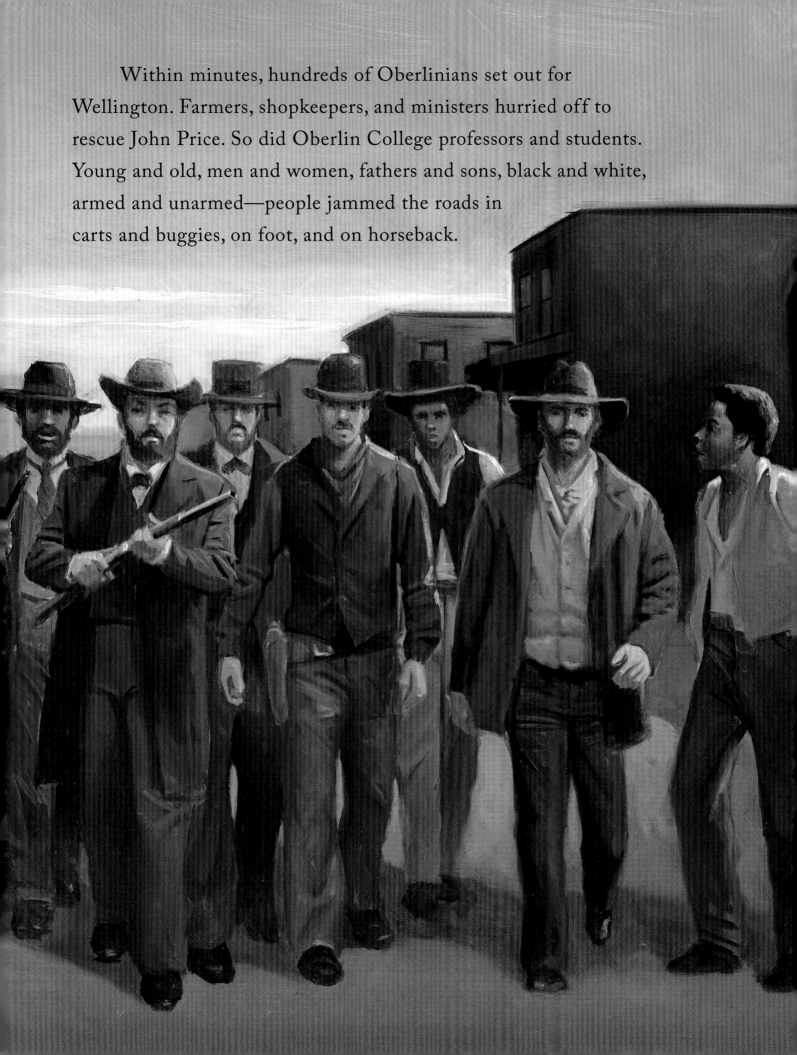

James Fitch and his clerk, Simeon Bushnell, closed their bookstore and dashed off to Wellington.

Henry and Wilson Bruce Evans hurried off from their cabinet shop. The Evans brothers were married to sisters and had eleven children between them.

Oberlin student William Lincoln was in his room when some classmates pounded on his door. He was the man to rescue John Price, they told him, offering him a gun. Lincoln hated slavery, but he also hated violence. Unsure what to do, he knelt on the floor with his Bible and asked himself: "If it were your own brother, what would you do?"

His answer? "Rescue him or die!" Lincoln grabbed the gun and raced to Wellington.

Several rescuers were former slaves, willing to risk their
own freedom for justice. Charles Langston, who had become a
schoolteacher, headed to Wellington. Langston was dedicated to
ending slavery and was an Ohio State Anti-Slavery Society official.
John Scott, who owned a harness store in Oberlin, quickly got

ready to join the rescue party. "We'll get him!" Scott said. Taking three rifles from his shop, he drove a buggy to Wellington along with two passengers.

John Watson sped away from his ice cream parlor/grocery by wagon. His nineteen-year-old son, William, a store clerk who had attended Oberlin College, followed him to Wellington.

3:00 p.m.

As hundreds of Oberlinians surrounded Wadsworth's Hotel, Wellington residents joined them. They included Matthew Gillet, a seventy-four-year-old farmer and Underground Railroad conductor.

"Father" Gillet was the oldest of the Rescuers, as the crowd that gathered to free John Price became known.

"Bring him out!" the crowd chanted. "Bring him out!"

Through the attic window, Anderson Jennings saw that he and his men were vastly outnumbered. Still, they had one huge advantage: the law. Jennings stepped onto the hotel balcony. "This boy is mine by the laws of Kentucky and of the United States!" he said, reminding the crowd that according to the Fugitive Slave Law they could be jailed for helping a slave escape.

Someone in the crowd hollered back, "There are no slaves
in Ohio and never will be!" When Jennings said that John didn't mind
returning to Kentucky, the crowd demanded that John come out to
the balcony to speak for himself.

"I suppose I've got to go back to Kentucky," John told the crowd.
What else could the captive say?

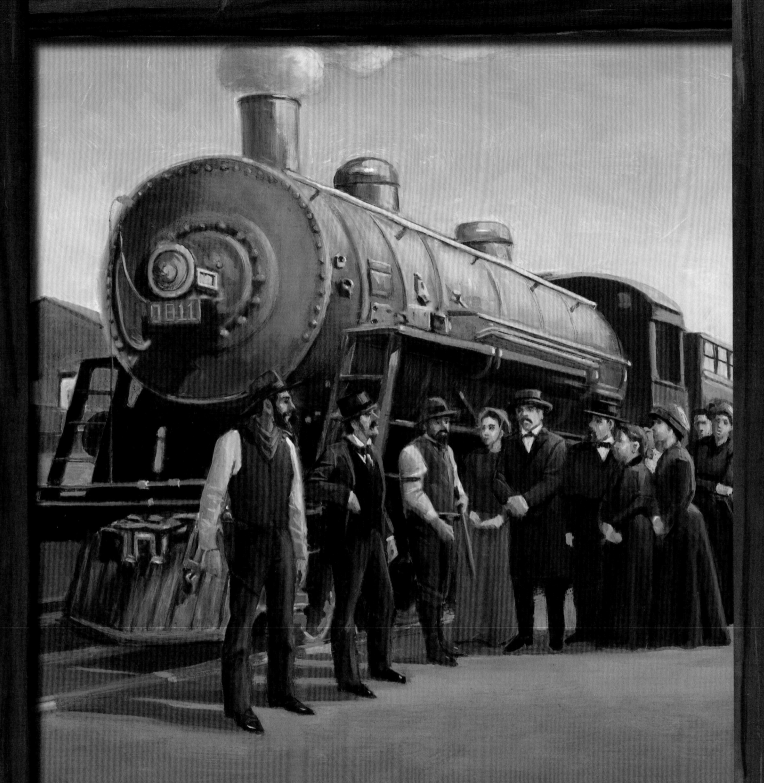

5:30 p.m.

The 5:13 train had arrived, but Jennings did not attempt to take John to the depot. A rumor swept through the crowd that the 8:00 p.m. train would bring soldiers to arrest John Price and return him to slavery. It was getting dark. The time for talk was over, the crowd murmured.

6:15 p.m.

A dozen men entered Wadsworth's Hotel. William Lincoln led a few of them, including Ansel Lyman, up the front stairs. John Scott led several men, including the Evans brothers and Charles Langston, up the narrow back stairway.

Guards posted by Jennings tried to stop Lincoln, Scott, and their men. Fistfights broke out. One of John Scott's men fired his gun at a guard who was blocking the stairway. Scott pushed the gun barrel upward—just in time. Instead of killing the guard, the bullet hit the ceiling.

The two groups joined together in the hallway outside the attic where John was being held. Within a few minutes they had John Price in their grasp. The Rescuers carried him downstairs, where bookstore clerk Simeon Bushnell drove him away in John Scott's buggy.

Bushnell took John Price to James Fitch's home, where he spent the night in a secret room. But the bookstore owner was too well known as an Underground Railroad worker for John to be safe there. Price was next taken to the home of Oberlin College mathematics professor James Fairchild.

"You must never tell anyone in the world that John is here," Mary Fairchild warned the couple's six children. They were doing the right thing by breaking an evil law, she explained, but if word that John was there leaked out, their father might be arrested.

John Price stayed with the Fairchilds for several days. Then he vanished. Some said he went to Canada. What became of Dinah and Frank also remains unknown.

The freeing of John Price became known as the Oberlin-Wellington Rescue. Opponents of slavery called the Rescuers heroes and Anderson Jennings and his men Kidnappers. Most Southerners considered the Rescuers criminals for breaking the Fugitive Slave Law.

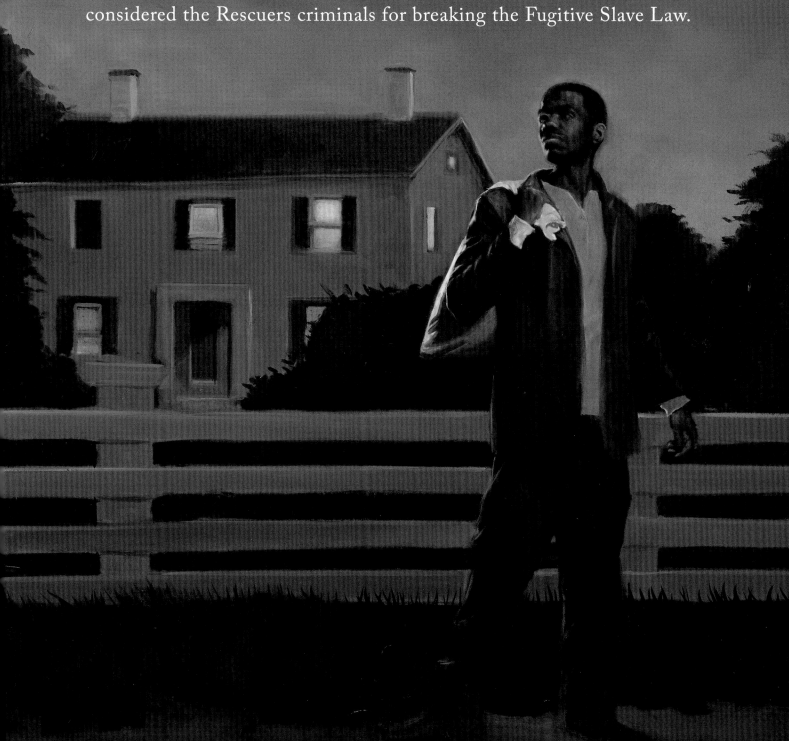

President James Buchanan sided with the slaveholders. He wanted to make an example of the Rescuers for defying the Fugitive Slave Law. The US government charged thirty-seven men with helping John Price escape. Among them was William Lincoln, who was teaching in Dublin, Ohio, when two law officers burst into his schoolroom.